For Leo and Arielle Ghiloni—always remember to
kiss your monsters. —L. F.

To my lovely mother, Carmelinda, who did a wonderful job
raising six little monsters. —M. R.

STERLING CHILDREN'S BOOKS
New York

An Imprint of Sterling Publishing
1166 Avenue of the Americas
New York, NY 10036

Text © 2015 by Lane Fredrickson
Illustrations © 2015 by Michael Robertson
Art direction and design by Merideth Harte

ISBN 978-1-4549-1345-0

Distributed in Canada by Sterling Publishing
c/o Canadian Manda Group, 664 Annette Street
Toronto, Ontario, Canada M6S 2C8
Distributed in the United Kingdom by GMC Distribution Services
Castle Place, 166 High Street, Lewes, East Sussex, England BN7 1XU
Distributed in Australia by Capricorn Link (Australia) Pty. Ltd.
P.O. Box 704, Windsor, NSW 2756, Australia

For information about custom editions, special sales, and premium and corporate purchases,
please contact Sterling Special Sales at 800-805-5489 or specialsales@sterlingpublishing.com.

Manufactured in China
Lot #:
2 4 6 8 10 9 7 5 3 1
6/15

www.sterlingpublishing.com/kids

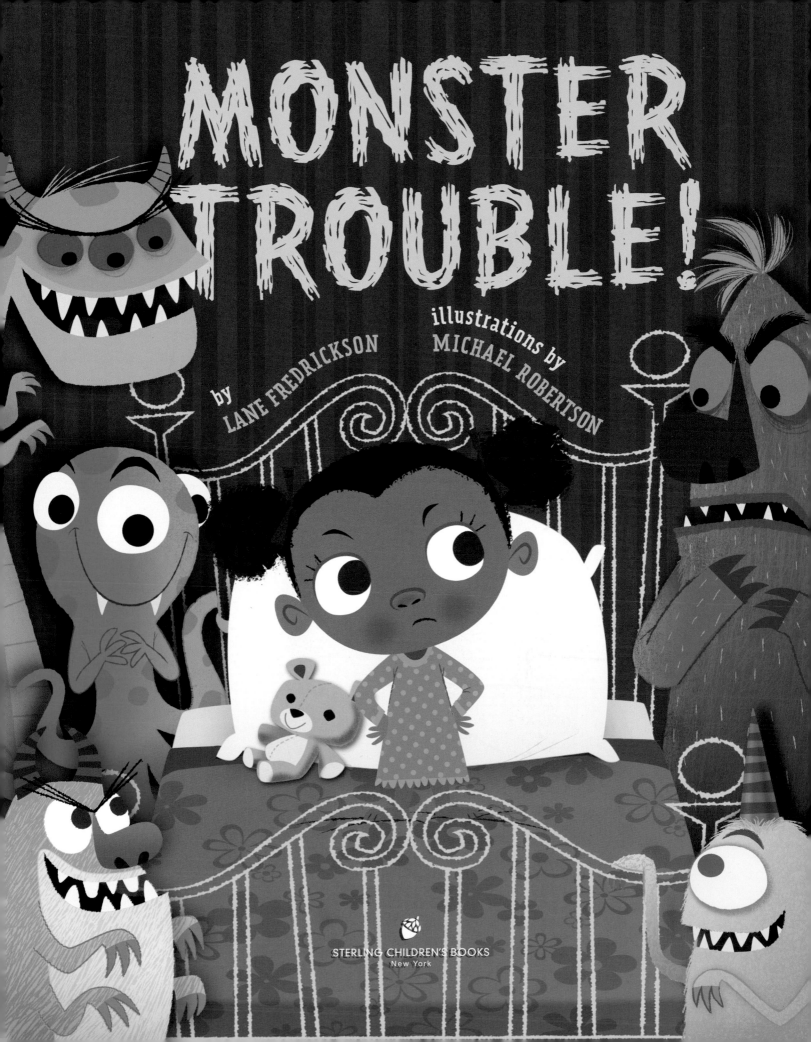

MONSTER TROUBLE!

by LANE FREDRICKSON

illustrations by MICHAEL ROBERTSON

STERLING CHILDREN'S BOOKS
New York

Winifred Schnitzel was never afraid.
Not of monsters or ghouls or the noises they made.

She loved scary movies and werewolves and thunder
and peg-legged pirates who bury their plunder.

Still, Winifred's bedtime was hardly spook-free.
The neighborhood monsters would *not* let her be.

Each night they'd show up and attempt to be scary.
Some would growl; some would belch. Some were slimy, some hairy.

But all of their monsterly mayhem was moot—
because Winifred Schnitzel thought monsters were cute.

Still, night after night, all those monsters kept creeping
into Winifred's room, interrupting her sleeping.

Too tired for math, too exhausted for fun,
she finally decided, "Those monsters are done!"

She ordered a book titled *Monsters Beware!* and constructed the "Sticky-String, Small Monster Snare."

But *that* night, the BIG monsters all showed up first;
the Sticky-String Snare got so stretched that it burst.

Winifred barely got through the next day.
She dozed off in art class and snoozed through ballet.

She decided, "That's it! I've got to get tough!"
She was tired of monsters. Enough was enough.

So she brought in some stinky, old Limburger cheese.
The label said: Caution! Makes Big Monsters Sneeze.

The monsters just called up the Goblin Street Deli.
They ordered in bagels and fish-eyeball jelly.

There were monsters on bed posts and stuck to the wall.
They made slingshots from string: They were having a ball.

Winifred sighed. They were louder than ever.
She knew that she needed to try something clever.

So she built every spook-trap in *Monsters Beware!*
and one of her own called "The Prickly Bum Chair."

Poor Winifred yawned. She was so very sleepy.
She was starting to look a bit spookishly creepy.

When the monsters showed up with their howling and roaring,
Winifred Schnitzel was already snoring!

She was dreaming of puppies when a monster went HISS.
She reached out and gave it a big, sleepy KISS.

The monster yelled, "Yuck!" All the others were heaving.
One gagged. And a big monster shouted, "I'm leaving!"

Winifred knew that despite their uniqueness,
she'd discovered that monsters have one silly weakness.

So she puckered and pouted and kissed them all good.
Those monsters screamed, running as fast as they could.

Now Winifred sleeps very soundly at night.
In the daytime, she's happy and perky and bright.

But sometimes she finds that a monster's crept in
right around bedtime, with a monsterly grin.

She ignores all the growling and roaring and hissing,
since the one thing that all monsters hate most is . . .

KISSING!